I0556747

COSMIC CARDIO

Once Upon a Bite #2

Charity Parkerson

Punk & Sissy Publications

COPYright

—Warning: This book is intended for readers over the age of 18. Some of my books contain allusions to past abuse and trauma. I try to have nothing triggering on page and treat every situation with care.

Editor: BZ Hercules & Consultants

CHARITY PARKERSON

Cover art: TMT Cover Design

contents

INTRODUCTION

COSMOS FEELS LIKE HE'S just found himself. Then a young vamp rips everything away from him. Now he must get his revenge.

In his twenties, Cosmos fluttered around, doing every odd job imaginable. Only recently has he discovered his passion: fitness. He's started his spin class, Cosmic Cardio, and—for the first time—everything in his life feels complete. Until one bite at a club ruins everything. Now, there's only one thing Cosmos can do to reclaim his pride. He has to find the vampire who bit him and destroy his life.

When Vega's ex left him with a teenaged son years ago, he thought being a single dad would be his biggest challenge. Then his son came home a vampire. Now his son won't stop turning people against their will. When Cosmos shows up angry and bent on teaching his son a lesson, Vega is just fed up enough to let it happen. After all, it's not like Cosmos plans to kill him. He simply intends to marry Vega and be the step-vampire from hell. Vega has already had one nightmare marriage. At least Cosmos intends to co-parent. What does he have to lose? Only maybe his heart. That's nothing he hasn't lost before.

COSMIC CARDIO

Cosmic Cardio is the second book in Charity Parkerson's Once Upon a Bite series. These books are meant to be short, fun paranormal romps to brighten your day.

CHAPTER ONE

THERE WAS THIS PLACE downtown. Only the freaks went there. Cosmos was aware there was a song out there that warned of such places. It was every bit as dirty as billed. Cosmos loved it. People fucked on the dance floor. In the bathrooms. There was no shame. That was Cosmos' jam. He was a free spirit. His parents had been too. Obviously. They had named him Cosmos, after all. They had split when he turned eighteen. Yep. They had jumped in their flower-painted van and waved goodbye, leaving him behind with six months' rent and zero life skills. Even though they had said they would be back after getting some traveling out of their blood, it hadn't happened. He had known it wouldn't. To be honest, Cosmos couldn't believe they made it until he was eighteen. They had never been very good at being adults. He wasn't either, but he tried harder than they had. Except for this one part of his life. He loved this club.

"Would you like to dance?"

A wicked smile pulled at Cosmos' lips. "I fucking love to dance." Cosmos allowed himself to get dragged onto the dance floor.

The young twenty-something was just his type. Blond. Lithe. All smiles. He was also obviously up for a good time. That was all Cosmos wanted because Cosmos was currently focusing on himself. He wasn't looking to get tied down... well, not figuratively. Literally, that was a different story. Literally, that was still on the table. Otherwise, he didn't care who asked him to dance or what they did afterward, as long as it was a good time. He was all about the good time right now. Cosmos had goals.

The blond held his stare as they moved with the beat of the music. He wore a knowing smile, and that shit was hot as hell. Confidence always took Cosmos to his knees faster than any compliment would. The guy was young. He couldn't be over twenty-one. Honestly, that was for the best. Not because Cosmos preferred them younger than him, but because younger men didn't want anything serious.

"You should probably tell me now if there's anything you aren't willing to do."

Fuck. Confidence. Yum. "You sound pretty certain I'm willing to do anything at all."

"You're here. You're dancing." He snagged Cosmos' hips and hauled him closer until the lower halves of their bodies met. "And you're hard."

Cosmos didn't blush. He wasn't ashamed. This was why he was here. "I don't even know your name."

"You can call me... Apollo."

A smile snapped to Cosmos' lips. There was something alluring about Apollo. His eyes caught the barely existent light inside the club and reflected it back to Cosmos, mesmerizing him. Cosmos felt like he was falling deeper into Apollo's eyes. The music faded. It got farther away as Apollo moved closer. A vague sense of something not being quite right overcame Cosmos. He realized they were outside, but he didn't recall leaving the club. The stench of back-alley trash overwhelmed him, pulling him from the moment.

"Look at me, Cosmos. Focus on me. On us. We're dancing." A hint of fang showed as Apollo made the claim. Full-blown panic hit.

"Um. No. I'm out. Ain't nobody making a vampire out of me tonight. I got aspirations."

Apollo snagged his arm before he could get away. "Stop being dramatic. We're just playing. I'm not turning anyone into a vampire. I thought you were down for anything."

"Not this." He tried again to pull away. A pain shot up his arm and through his head. Everything went dark.

A loud beeping startled Cosmos' eyes open. He immediately closed them again. The overwhelming stench of garbage made him gag. Tiny heartbeats pounded in his ears. The scurry of dozens of little feet was all around him. Cosmos' stomach heaved again. He tried harder to pry open his eyes. Concrete and trash surrounded him. A car alarm blared in the distance. To him, it sounded as if he had his ear pressed against the hood of the car. He forced himself to focus. Nothing looked familiar. Panic tried overtaking him. Then the vaguest memory sneaked in, followed by another. The taste of copper filled Cosmos' mouth. He gagged. This couldn't be happening. Not to him. He was always so careful. This couldn't be real. He felt of his pockets. A cry rattled in his throat when he found his phone still there. Cosmos pried it out of his tight jeans and squinted against the light it gave off as he scrolled through his contacts. When he found the name he was looking for, Cosmos hit the call icon and put the phone on speaker. He squeezed his eyes shut. A tear slid down his cheek as he listened to the phone ring.

"Hello?"

"Draco." Even Cosmos heard the heavy whine in his voice. He sniffed. It came out stuttered as his chest heaved. "I need you. This motherfucker done turned me into a vampire." Every word came out in a wail he couldn't control. It didn't matter he had someone he could call in this fucked-up situation. Cosmos felt he was entitled to at least a small breakdown. His life was over, after all.

CHAPTER TWO

OVER THE YEARS, COSMOS had done a lot of odd jobs on his hunt to find himself. At one time, he had worked at a blood bank. That was where he had met his best friend, Tate. Back then, Tate had been a hapless Little looking to survive by selling plasma. Now he was a secure Little with the perfect vampire dom daddy. All because Tate had been turned into a vampire in the same fucking club nearly eleven years ago. That should have been

Cosmos' cue to never go back, but it had been nearly eleven years and never once had he been vamped before now. Plus, Tate's husband Draco had ended the vampire that turned Tate, so Cosmos hadn't really thought much about it. Not to mention, what were the fucking odds?

It tracked, though, that the moment he got his life together would be the exact moment some bullshit like this sideswiped him. He was thirty-four and had just found his passion. Cosmos had just started his very own business, Cosmic Cardio. It was a spin class. He was a business owner. Him. Cosmos was pretty damn proud of that. He had worked hard as hell to find something that made him happy. Now that little fucker at the club had stolen everything. He couldn't make any money, only being open when the sun was down. Cosmos had sunk everything he had into his studio. The level of rage and pain he felt couldn't be soothed. Cosmos' life was ruined.

Tate sat nearby, wearing dinosaur pajamas and holding a teddy bear. His gaze followed Cosmos as Cosmos paced the floor nonstop. "Just tell us how we can help. Daddy and I will do anything you need. If you hadn't been there for me after I was bitten, I wouldn't have made it. You know there's nothing I won't do for you."

"Would you like me to kill him?" Draco asked, sounding calm and completely cool with murder.

Cosmos was too at this point. He flashed the pair a tight smile. "I love you both, and no. Death is too good for him. Too quick. I just need to figure out how to find him. Once I set eyes on him, then maybe I'll know what to do. Maybe I'll decide to kill him myself."

"You should feel him."

Cosmos' gaze shot to Tate. "What?"

Tate hugged his bear tighter, making Cosmos wonder exactly how intense he looked. Cosmos tried to tone it down for Tate's sake. Tate motioned Draco's way. "Even though Draco's blood is ancient, and the guy who turned you can't control you now that Draco's blood has overpowered his, you should still feel him. Just turn into a bat and follow that feeling."

A panic attack tried overtaking Cosmos. He forgot he could turn into a bat now. "I don't know how to do that. I don't want to be a flying rodent." Even Cosmos heard the screech in his voice. He couldn't help it. Too much was happening at once.

"A sky puppy," Tate corrected, sounding hurt and slightly indignant.

The last thing Cosmos wanted was to hurt Tate's feelings. Tate and Draco had dropped everything and shown up for him the instant he called. Draco had given him blood to burn off the power Apollo could choose to hold over him, and then the pair had stayed with him through the daylight hours. He didn't have anyone else. They were amazing. He was just stressed. Cosmos pinched the spot between his eyes and took a steadying breath. As he released the air from his lungs, he focused on the dark feeling that still lingered in his gut. He didn't know how he knew, but Cosmos knew that was Apollo... lurking.

"I'll take my bike."

With his eyes still closed and his senses guiding him, Cosmos headed outside and down the stairs to where his bike was chained outside his apartment building. He felt Draco and Tate following on his heels.

"Would you like us to go with you as protection?"

A smile that felt evil pulled at Cosmos' lips. His inner rage made him feel like he could take over the world. Likely he would need them later when he crashed. His life was still over. Cosmos' dreams were dead. For now, vengeance drove him.

"I'll call if I need you, but I've got this. That little bastard is mine." Cosmos moved to his bike and broke the chain that secured his bicycle to the bike rack. It crumbled in his hand like the steel rope was made of Legos. He jumped on and sped away without looking back. His entire being had one goal: finding his prey. He pedaled faster and faster until the streetlights looked like a singular white line in the corner of his eye as he zipped by. Wind whipped at his face. He could hear and smell everything. Cosmos had never felt more alive. He had no idea how fast he moved, but he wasn't even winded when he came to a screeching halt outside a single-family vinyl siding home at the end of a cul-de-sac.

It was blue. Even though it was pitch dark outside, with Cosmos' new night vision, he could see everything as if it was the middle of the day. He was a bit confused. The last thing he expected to find was a normal-looking house. He expected a rat bastard would live where snakes did. The place looked like a home for a married couple with two kids. It was perfectly landscaped, for fuck's sake. His prey was inside, though. Cosmos felt him and his rage hit the ceiling. His feet barely touched the grass as he levitated with anger on the march to the door. He rang the doorbell with such force, the button disappeared inside the doorframe. With a growl, Cosmos tried pulling back his newfound strength when he knocked. He only slightly dented the door.

The door opened.

Cosmos was ready to fight.

An older and sexier version of Apollo stood inside the doorway. He was human. Cosmos could smell it, and he didn't even know how he could tell the difference already, but he could. His eyes were light green, and fuck. That took some of the wind from his sails. So too did the adorable little laugh lines around his eyes. Just goddamn. He was hot.

"Yes?" He looked confused.

Cosmos squared his shoulders. He couldn't let himself get distracted by the yumminess. "Where is Apollo? I have a bone to pick with that little shit."

A deep line appeared between the hottie's eyebrows. "There's no one here by that name."

COSMIC CARDIO

A hysterical burble of laughter escaped Cosmos before he could call it back. "Oh, he's here. I can feel him."

The blond's expression didn't clear. "I don't know what that means."

Cosmos held his hand out to eye level. "This tall. Blond. Looks like you. Turned me into a goddamn vampire." Cosmos shouted the last words at the top of lungs because he couldn't stop.

"Oh, dear. Not again."

Cosmos' eyes widened, trying to bug from his head. "Not again? What the fuck do you mean, not again? How are you saying that like this happens once a week?"

The man swiped a shaking hand over his eyes. He looked tired when he focused on Cosmos again. "I'm Vega," he said, touching his chest. That was kind of nice. Fuck. Cosmos was not in the mood to ooh and ahh over this dude. Vega motioned behind him. "Please, come in so we can talk."

Oh, Cosmos was coming in all right. He planned to rip out a throat tonight. He stepped inside, trying to hold on to his dignity. He looked around. Apollo wasn't in sight, but Cosmos still felt him, though. The place was nice. It had a burgundy leather loveseat and couch and smelled like apples. Someone obviously tried to make the place a home for a psychopath who apparently turned people into vampires every other day.

Vega motioned toward the loveseat. "Have a seat."

Cosmos ignored the offer. "Where's Apollo?"

"His name is Aaron, not Apollo. He's barely eighteen."

Cosmos sat, mostly because his knees gave out. "What?"

Vega nodded. He chose the seat across from Cosmos. "Aaron, my son, he got turned about a year ago. Before then, I had no idea any of this was real. Obviously, I can't control him. I'm a single dad. He barely listened to me before he became invincible, but now..." A sad smile touched Vega's lips. "Sorry. I don't know why I said all that. You're obviously in a much worse position than me, and I don't even know your name."

"Cosmos."

A breathtaking smile stretched Vega's lips. "That's nice. We both either had astronomers or hippies for parents."

"Hippies," they both said simultaneously, and then smiled.

Cosmos' smile fell. He covered his eyes for a second. A wave of hopelessness washed over him. "I was so close to finally being the adult I always wanted in my life." A stuttered-sounding breath escaped Cosmos. "I finally had my own business. Now what will I do? Goddamn it."

"Fuck, Dad. Keep it down in here. I'm trying to—oh."

Cosmos shot to his feet as Aaron strolled into the living room, barking orders at

Vega and acting the prick. His temper returned full force. "Well, look who it is."

Aaron visibly swallowed.

Cosmos snarled.

Aaron's shoulders squared, as if he recalled he held all the power. "Come to find your maker, eh? Don't bother. I'm not really interested. You're too old for me."

An evil-sounding chuckle rose in Cosmos' throat. He knew he had to look every bit as deadly as he felt. "Oh, don't worry. I'm not here for you."

Aaron blinked. "You're not?"

Just as Cosmos hoped, now that he was here, he knew exactly what to do. It wasn't good enough to kill the little shit who'd ruined his life—and apparently several others—Cosmos needed to wreck him. "Oh, no. I am not." Cosmos dragged out every word. "See, I didn't realize last night, since you were in a kink club—"

"You were in a kink club?" Vega asked behind him, sounding upset.

Cosmos ignored him. "I didn't realize how young you are since you have to be twenty-one to get in."

Aaron smirked. "It's nothing to mind-control the guys at the door. In fact, I can control anyone I want." He glanced past Cosmos. "Dad, jump on one foot."

Cosmos looked over his shoulder. "Don't do that."

COSMIC CARDIO

Aaron looked more than a little stunned when Vega obeyed Cosmos and not him. "Dad, I said—"

Cosmos held up his hand.

Aaron grabbed his throat, looking confused as to why words failed him. Cosmos smirked as he continued choking Aaron's voice away from across the room. "Here's how it'll be. I'm going to fuck your dad."

"What?"

Cosmos ignored the squeaked question behind him. Instead, his evil smile grew as he advanced on Aaron. "That's right. The very first thing I'm going to do is fuck the hell out of your dad, because," he glanced behind him and eyed Vega from head to toe, "that man is hella fine. Damn, I'm glad I didn't end up touching you last night because... wow. He's ten times the man you are." Cosmos went back to staring at Aaron with all the madness in his soul. "I don't plan to stop there. Nope. You've already ruined my future, so you know what? I'm marrying your dad. That's right. Say hello to your new stepdad, because it's way past time someone got you under control. You're about to find out today."

Aaron fought past his control. He growled through gritted teeth, "I own you. You're not touching my dad."

A laugh that sounded insane, even to Cosmos' ears, exploded from his lips and reverberated from the walls. "You don't own shit. You picked the wrong motherfucking witch, asshole. When you chose me, you should've looked a little closer because I've got them good connections." Cosmos stabbed himself in the chest with his finger, emphasizing every word. "You done fucked up A A Ron. That's right, I know your real name now. I called up my best friend, and he got his daddy Draco to fix me up with that ancient blood."

Aaron's eyes widened. "You know Draco?"

Satisfaction roared through Cosmos. "You're damn right I do, so you hear me now. First," he held up one finger. "I fuck your dad. Second," he held up a second finger. "I make you my stepson. Third," he held up only his middle finger, flipping Aaron the bird. "I watch every move you make, and if you even think about turning another human, I'm breaking my foot off in your ass."

Aaron's chin jutted out. "You're forgetting something in this grand plan of yours. My dad has to go along with it."

"I'm not forgetting shit." He pointed at himself. "Ancient blood. Mind control."

"Wait. Hold up. There's no need for that."

Cosmos glanced behind him at the calmly spoken words. "Do you want to fuck?"

Vega squared his shoulders. "Yes. I think I do."

Cosmos turned back Aaron's way with an evil smile stretching his lips so wide it hurt. "Do you plan to stay to watch?" He slapped his thighs. "I've got amazing thighs. After all, I had my own spin class before you ruined my fucking life." Cosmos bounced up and down and moved his hips. "I can ride your daddy all night long."

"Oh my God. No. My eyes."

Satisfaction roared through Cosmos as Aaron ran for what he assumed was his bedroom. Maybe it was only the beginning of his revenge, but it felt amazing. He couldn't stop smiling.

For the past year... no. Since Aaron turned sixteen and Terry left for some guy he met online, Vega had been barely hanging on to his sanity. Aaron hadn't stopped acting out, then he came home a goddamn vampire and the real nightmare had begun. Vega had been mourning the loss of a twenty-year relationship and the son he once knew. He felt like a prisoner in his own home because he never knew what Aaron would do next. Aaron could make him do anything he chose. Vega never slept anymore. He lived in constant fear.

Now this livid yet beautiful stranger had burst into his life, looking like fucking salvation. Vega couldn't look away from him. His dark hair was a mess—like he had been running his fingers through it for hours. Vega imagined that was from the stress. He had the lightest blue eyes Vega had ever seen. Each time they swung Vega's way, his knees weakened.

"Thank you."

Those gorgeous eyes focused on him again. "For what? I wasn't joking. I meant every word I said."

Butterflies stirred in Vega's gut. He should be scared. Vega should definitely tell Cosmos to leave. Everything about this was insane. But for the first time in years, he didn't feel like he was facing everything alone. Maybe that was ridiculous, but he was so tired. "I know you did."

Cosmos' gaze dropped to Vega's mouth. He looked hungry. No one had looked at him with lust in years. He'd felt old and undesirable for so fucking long. "I didn't know about you before I got here. You can say no. I'd never take away anyone's free will the way mine was stripped from me. You're very sexy."

A blush exploded through Vega's face. "You don't have to say that. I know this is about Aaron, and I still agree. Something has to be done. I'm out of ideas. I need help."

Cosmos took a step closer. Vega pressed a hand to his stomach. He was sexual in a way Vega had never encountered. "I can smell your lust. It's changed your blood. Sweetened it. It's odd. I swear my tongue already knows your taste. You're wrong, by the way. This isn't just about Aaron. It was when I got here. Then I saw you. You should touch me."

He wasn't as bold as Cosmos. It had been a long time since he touched anyone... since anyone touched him. In a flash, Cosmos closed the distance between them. Vega blinked and Cosmos was across the room. Despite living with a vampire, he never got used to the unnatural speed.

"You're nervous."

A shy smile tugged at Vega's lips. He couldn't deny it.

Cosmos unexpectedly stroked Vega's bottom lip. "It's okay. I'm a stranger. You're not like me."

Vega tore his gaze from Cosmos' lips to focus on his gorgeous eyes. "What do you mean?"

Cosmos smirked. "Shameless."

God help him. Vega's knees weakened. He automatically gripped Cosmos' t-shirt, searching for purchase. "I was with the same man for a long time, and I haven't been with anyone since he left."

Vega didn't know what it was about Cosmos. He just couldn't stop baring his soul. "You're hypnotizing."

Cosmos blinked and took a step back, pulling out of Vega's hold. "I'm sorry. I don't know when I'm using my charms. It's literally my first full day as a vampire. You don't deserve this."

Something about Cosmos' sudden vulnerability emboldened Vega. He moved closer. "It wasn't anything unnatural mesmerizing me. You're gorgeous."

A sweet smile touched Cosmos' lips, making Vega want to take care of him. "Why don't we sit down? Let's just talk for a minute."

Cosmos nodded and reclaimed his spot on the loveseat. This time, Vega joined him. He turned slightly so he could meet Cosmos' stare. No matter how hard he tried, Vega couldn't tear his gaze away from Cosmos. It honestly hurt his chest, thinking about what Aaron had stolen from him. This man had an entire life somewhere before Aaron carelessly kicked it over like a sandcastle on the beach. Vega wanted to make right what he could.

"Tell me about your business."

Cosmos smiled. Vega swore he felt the pride rolling off him. "It's just a small space in a strip mall near downtown. But I sank everything I had into the place. It's a spin class that focuses on fun rather than fitness goals, so people don't get frustrated. I play loud music and we have classes with bubbles and flashing lights.

Sometimes it's like a rave but for exercise. Other times, it's slower-paced for beginners. It's called Cosmic Cardio." The more Cosmos talked about his business, the more animated he became. Then his smile melted away. "But it's as good as failed now. I can't make enough money to keep the doors open by only having one or two classes a night and the daylight hours are lost to me now. Plus, my client list already wasn't that big. I was already barely making ends meet since I was just getting my name out there. But things were really picking up, you know? For the first time, I genuinely thought I'd be good at something."

Vega's hand moved without thinking. He swept Cosmo's hair behind his ear. Vega was a fixer by nature. He needed to comfort Cosmos. "I get the feeling you could never fail at anything. You just need a second to breathe and think. I know we just met, and you don't have any reason to believe in me, but—back in the day—I used to have a pretty impressive list of businesses I helped get off the ground. That was all before I retired to become a stay-at-home dad, but the knowledge is still in there," he said, touching his head. "If you let me help you brainstorm, I bet we could find a way to keep the doors open."

Cosmos smiled. There was no happiness in the gesture. "You're really nice." He stood. "I hope your son realizes how good he has it before it's too late. It was nice meeting you."

A wave of hopelessness washed over Vega. "Oh. Okay." He dropped his gaze to his lap. His throat burned. At some point in his life, he had become this undesirable thing worth nothing to anyone, yet he still got up every day and kept going. He was just someone's dad and someone's ex. That was it. He was invisible.

Unexpectedly, Cosmos dropped to his knees between Vega's feet, where he could see Vega's face. He dipped beneath Vega's lowered chin and pressed a quick kiss to Vega's lips before pulling away.

Vega's chin shot up.

From his spot on his knees, Cosmos held his gaze. For a moment, neither of them moved. Then everything exploded. He didn't know which of them moved first, but they came together in a fury of passion. Cosmos bit Vega's bottom lip and held on as he dove both hands beneath Vega's shirt.

Vega pushed, taking Cosmos to the floor. When their tongues finally stroked, a loud moan tore from Vega. It was out of his control. He heard something rip. Cool air brushed his back, and he realized Cosmos had literally torn off his shirt. Vega had never felt more desired. He felt reckless and... free. Young. It had been years since he had acted in pure lust. He couldn't stop touching Cosmos. It was beyond obvious Cosmos taught fitness for a living. His body was flawless. Vega wanted to lick every inch.

"Your thoughts have me ready to come in my jeans."

Vega froze. "You can read my thoughts?"

Cosmos winced. "I can't help it. You're kind of screaming them at me."

His gaze moved down Cosmos' body. His shirt was pushed halfway up his torso, showing off an adorable flat stomach. With messy hair, arousal written in every line of his expression, and unbuttoned jeans, Cosmos' image should have been plastered on the cover of every magazine. Vega's dick jumped.

"Yeah. I don't care if you can hear my thoughts. Goddamn. I've never wanted to fuck anyone so badly in my life."

A smile exploded across Cosmos' face. "We should probably find a bed. Don't you think?"

Even though his knees already hurt, Vega didn't care. He would stay on the floor forever if it meant he got to be inside Cosmos. But he needed lube and a condom. Horror struck. "Fuck. I don't have any condoms."

Cosmos snorted. "Your son killed me. I can't get or spread diseases any longer."

"Oh." Vega felt guilty for the relief that poured through him.

Cosmos stood, bringing Vega with him. "When it comes to this, don't feel guilty. Just take me to bed."

Vega took Cosmos' hand and headed for the open door of his bedroom. The next thing he knew, he was on his back on the mattress, nude, with Cosmos kissing his way down his body.

"Holy shit. I can't keep up."

Cosmos chuckled against his skin. "I'm just getting used to how fast I am now. Damn. You taste good." *I can hear your heart beating. Smell your lust. It's so sexy.*

"Um, did I just hear you inside my head?"

Cosmos sat back on his heels and looked around. "I don't know. Did you? Where's the lube?"

"The nightstand." Vega forgot his earlier question as he watched Cosmos crawl toward the bedside table. He was so flawless, he looked Photoshopped. Vega didn't think he had ever been that perfect, even when he had been in his twenties. He wanted to touch and lick every inch.

Cosmos found the lube. He made a show of wetting his asshole for Vega. Vega was panting by the time Cosmos straddled him.

"Yes. Please? Sit on my dick. You're so beautiful."

Cosmos held Vega's dick in place and slowly lowered himself. Vega's muscles clenched. His body bowed. He panted, trying not to immediately come when Cosmos made a sound that drew his balls up tight.

God. Yes. Destroy my hole.

"I heard you in my head again. If you keep thinking things like that, I won't last two minutes."

An evil-sounding chuckle vibrated from Cosmos. "So? Come. I bet I can make you come again and again. You won't be able to get hard again for days."

Vega gasped when Cosmos' body sped to moving too fast to see. An orgasm ripped through him. He didn't have time to recover before he was on the edge again and Cosmos was back to slowly rocking himself on Vega's cock.

"Damn, that's right, daddy. Make my ass leak. I'll be dripping cum for hours."

"Oh, God. What just happened?"

Cosmos' tongue filled his mouth. *You got fucked. Would you like it to happen again?*

The question had barely brushed Vega's mind before it happened again. Cosmos vibrated on his cock too fast to see, but another orgasm had him shaking, yet he was hard again and ready to go.

COSMIC CARDIO

With his hands buried in Cosmos' hair, Vega held on and sucked Cosmos' tongue. He took every orgasm Cosmos gave him until he had been wrung dry, and Cosmos cried out around their entwined tongues. His body tried sucking Vega deeper. Vega let Cosmos use him. He missed being touched and held. Kissed.

By the time Cosmos finally rolled to one side and snuggled against him, Vega swore he already lost part of himself. He was exhausted yet exhilarated. His hands kept roaming Cosmos' perfect body. Vega couldn't stop savoring the sensation of soft, flawless skin beneath his fingertips.

"I wasn't flawless before I turned."

Vega's gaze shot to Cosmos' face at the quietly spoken words. "What?"

Cosmos looked sad. He placed his hand over Vega's and dragged it down his torso to his lower abdomen. "I used to have a scar right here where I had my appendix removed." He brought Vega's hand to his mouth and kissed it before nuzzling it with his chin. "There was a deep white scar right here from where I fell at the skating rink when I was ten and caught myself with my face. It needed ten stitches. There were dozens of others. I just woke up someone else yesterday." Tears filled Cosmos' eyes as he made the claim.

Vega couldn't look away. His heart squeezed. All those marks had made up Cosmos' past. They had painted a canvas of who he was and now they were gone. Lost to him forever. Vega couldn't even imagine.

"Tell me how I can make it better."

A sweet smile touched Cosmos' lips. "You already have. You gave me my first happy vampire memory. That means more than you can know." Cosmos' eyes closed. His chest rose and fell with a deep breath. "The sun is coming. I can feel it."

Vega nodded. "I'll keep you safe."

Cosmos squeezed his hand, and Vega vowed he would keep his word. He would watch over Cosmos with his life, not only while he slept, but from now on. Cosmos deserved a partner in life. Not just because Aaron was responsible for his death, but because Vega felt something tugging in his chest when he looked at Cosmos. Vega had stopped believing in fate and happy endings a long time ago, but he trusted his instincts. His gut said Cosmos needed him as much as Vega needed Cosmos. Together, they would figure this out. Together, they would heal.

CHAPTER THREE

THE SCENT OF SOMETHING delicious pulled Cosmos from the bed. Too late, he realized he didn't have any clean clothes. Then he remembered how Tate had just made pajamas with his mind after he turned. Cosmos closed his eyes and gave it a shot. When his eyes opened again, he wore jeans and a black t-shirt. He bounced a little in his excitement. It turned out he wasn't completely useless. With his body sufficiently covered, Cosmos followed his nose. The sound of a steady heartbeat got louder as the yummy smell got closer. Vega stood at the kitchen counter. Cosmos floated to him, searching for the scent until his nose was buried in the crook of Vega's neck.

He inhaled. "Oh, my God. Something smells amazing." His mouth filled with saliva and his fangs grew. It was out of his control.

Vega laughed as Cosmos nuzzled him. "I'm making a fruit tray. Would you like some? Oh. Shit. Sorry. I forgot you don't eat now."

A gasp escaped Cosmos as Vega's words slapped him with reality. He jumped backward. "Holy shit. It's you. You smell like that." He covered his mouth.

Vega turned. He looked slightly bemused when he should have been terrified.

"It's you," Cosmos whispered behind his hand.

"Oh. You're probably hungry."

He said the words so casually while Cosmos was mortified.

Cosmos spoke behind his hand to keep from scaring Vega with his fangs. "I'm sorry. I'm having a bit of an existential crisis right now. Just give me a second."

A sexy chuckle rumbled from the back of Vega's throat. He set the knife he'd been using to cut the fruit aside and motioned Cosmos forward. "Come here."

Cosmos shook his head. "I don't want to hurt you."

Sexy green eyes leveled a very adult-like look at him, making him feel ridiculous. "Stop being dramatic. You won't hurt me. Now come here."

"Damn. Lucky for you, I love a bossy man," Cosmos muttered as he shuffled Vega's way.

Vega snagged his hips and hauled him close. "Now you obviously had to bite someone to survive before you met me, right?"

Cosmos nodded.

"So you know how it's done, right?"

Cosmos nodded again.

Vega smiled. "All right, then. You've got this. How do you feel the most comfort-able? Aaron's only bitten me on the wrist in the past." Vega's gaze moved down Cosmos' body. "But it's you, so..."

Cosmos' stomach growled. He swore his fangs itched. Cosmos slid the fruit tray aside and lifted Vega onto the counter. This new strength was freeing in a way he hadn't expected. Cosmos had always been into looking good, but he had never wanted to be one of those buff guys. Being strong, though... it was kind of a power move. He loved the way the air instantly changed around Vega. The lust that immediately stirred made his hunger grow. Cosmos pushed Vega's shorts up his thighs, exposing the vein he wanted. He held Vega's stare as he bent and went down on him. When he struck, Vega moaned. His fingers found Cosmos' hair and held on—like he enjoyed it. Cosmos sucked.

Vega whimpered. "Oh, my God. I'm going to come."

"Gross, guys. You have a bedroom. I'm going to find me a snack." The front door slammed before Cosmos mustered the will to retract his fangs.

He smelled Vega's cum.

A flush rode high on Vega's cheeks as he stared at Cosmos, fighting for air. Regret washed over him. He wanted so badly to take Vega to bed. "I have to follow him."

Vega nodded. "I know."

"I'll be back, though."

Vega nodded. "I know."

Cosmos pressed a quick kiss to Vega's lips and zipped out the door, leaving something new and powerful behind. He didn't understand what just happened between them, but it was nice. Cosmos wanted to do it again. First, he needed to make sure Aaron didn't hurt anyone. Then he had a spin class tonight. But after that, he would show Vega he wasn't just hanging around for no reason. Cosmos really liked him. He was the only silver lining in Cosmos' otherwise bleak new world. That meant something. Possibly, it meant everything.

Vega took a quick shower. He needed a moment to hide his humiliation. Vega hadn't come in his clothes like that in decades. Everything about Cosmos was just... wow. He blew Vega away. Vega had spent the day thinking about Cosmos' plight. He shouldn't have to suffer because of Aaron. The way Cosmos had sounded when he talked about his business made Vega's chest hurt. Vega hadn't experienced that much passion about anything in years, but he recalled exactly what it felt like to have all his dreams ripped away by an uncaring stranger. If Vega could fix this, he would. They would start tonight.

While still towel-drying his hair, a cool body molded against his back. Firm lips touched his shoulder and spoke against his skin. "He behaved."

Vega nodded. He was more relieved than Cosmos could know. "Thank you."

Cosmos kissed his neck. "I have a spin class scheduled tonight. Afterward, if you want, I can come back."

"Actually." Vega turned in Cosmos' arms. "Can I go with you to your spin class? I'd love to see the place." His gaze moved down Cosmos' body. "I'd love to see you in action."

Cosmos stared at Vega's mouth, looking lost—like he wasn't listening. He nodded. "Anything you want."

"Good." That was good because he wanted Cosmos. Vega already had a plan brewing to help him with his business and to give him an excuse to spend more time with him.

"I need to leave soon."

Vega nodded and forced himself to take a step back. Cosmos kept him mesmerized. He didn't think it was magic related. It was just Cosmos. Vega wanted him like he had craved no one in years. The rush was addictive. "Just let me get my shoes."

Cosmos nodded.

"I'll drive."

Cosmos nodded again.

Vega fought a sigh. He wanted to drop to his knees.

"I can still hear your thoughts."

A hot blush exploded across Vega's face. He rushed to grab his shoes. A shameless-sounding chuckle followed on his heels. Vega stamped into his shoes and tried not to think. Cosmos unexpectedly snagged his throat and held him in place.

COSMIC CARDIO

All Vega could do was watch as Cosmos' mouth came down on his. His stomach muscles clenched. Their tongues entwined. Vega's knees weakened. Cosmos bit Vega's bottom lip before leaning away. He held Vega's stare, looking hungry. "Give me two hours to work, okay? Then the rest of the night I'm yours to do with as you please. Promise."

Vega couldn't look away from Cosmos' gorgeous eyes. He had spent twenty years with the same man and yet no one had had ever shaken him the way Cosmos had done in two days. "Tell me what's happening between us."

Cosmos smirked. "You're mine now. You feel it in your soul. Do you think a man named Vega met a man named Cosmos on accident? I don't. I'm still angry with

Aaron, and I'm upset about my business, but I'm not oblivious to you. Everything happens for a reason. I think you're my reason."

Damn. That was the hottest thing anyone had ever said to him. Vega would make sure Cosmos didn't lose his business and found a way to be happy in his new existence if it was the last thing he did. There was no other outcome as far as Vega was concerned. He needed Cosmos settled so they could focus on what was happening between them. Vega couldn't think about anything else.

"Work," Cosmos reminded him.

A smile snapped to Vega's lips. Cosmos made him forget everything. He shook his head and grabbed his keys. "All I need is an address."

Cosmos rattled off an address as Vega led the way to his older model Silverado. He knew the neighborhood and easily found Cosmos' little studio. It was cute. There was a neon pink sign. The place looked upbeat. Women and men were already lined up outside, waiting for Cosmos to unlock the door. Vega hung back and watched as Cosmos bounced from person to person, asking about kids and pets. He knew everyone's names without struggling. Vega's pride grew by the second.

"Hey, I'm Maggie."

Vega glanced over at the red-haired lady who interrupted his thoughts. "Hi. Vega." He held out his hand to shake.

She accepted his hand. "Nice to meet you. I haven't seen you here before. Is this your first time taking Cosmos' class?"

"Oh. I'm not here to take the class." Vega lifted weights and jogged occasionally, but stationary bikes weren't his thing. "Cosmos has to cut back the hours he's open, so I'm here to observe and help him find a way to make a profit with fewer hours."

Maggie looked taken aback. "Oh. I hope everything is okay."

Shit. Vega had spoken without thinking.

It's fine. Vega's shoulders relaxed as the words brushed his mind.

Cosmos appeared at his side. "Hey, Maggie. I see you've met my man."

COSMIC CARDIO

A bright smile lit Maggie's face. "Oh, my gosh. I didn't realize that's who this was." Her gaze moved between them. "You two are so gorgeous together and look so happy. I swear you look ten years younger, Cosmos."

Cosmos chuckled. "I'm happier than I've ever been."

She clapped while bouncing on her toes. "Love is so adorable."

Cosmos' gaze slid Vega's way. He winked. Vega bit back a laugh. He was ridiculously happy just existing in the same space as Cosmos. Vega prayed the feeling never ended. Cosmos wasn't the only one hoping to cling to a dream. While Cosmos wanted to keep his spin class, Vega needed to keep him. They were two fools life hadn't beaten yet. Together, Vega felt sure they could do anything.

His first spin class after the turn was interesting, to say the least. Doing anything at a human pace no longer came naturally. Thankfully, Vega sat in the corner and held Cosmos' stare throughout the entire class, keeping him in check. Each time Cosmos' speed became the least bit unnatural, Vega made a subtle gesture, motioning for him to bring it down a notch. Cosmos never would have made it through the class without him.

Afterward, Vega helped him clean up while looking thoughtful. "I had an idea, but I'm not sure how you feel about it."

Cosmos snagged Vega's waist. "Spill. I'm open to any suggestion at this point." He kissed Vega's neck before setting him free again.

With a bemused-looking smile, Vega moved to the next bike and wiped it down. "How do you feel about doing virtual classes? People could follow along online, and you wouldn't be limited to only local members."

Cosmos blinked. He hadn't thought of that. "That's... I mean, it's a great idea, but I don't know how to go about even getting started. I can't video myself and I know nothing about editing or uploading. I'm not very video tech savvy. But wow.

That's brilliant." The idea grew on him by the second. "If we could find someone who knows anything about the technology side of things, that could be huge."

Vega smiled. Cosmos felt his pride. He was glad he could help. Cosmos accidentally heard that thought without having to look. But that had Cosmos probing at Vega's thoughts on the sly. Vega genuinely wanted to see Cosmos succeed. It was important to him. He wanted Cosmos to be happy and be a part of his life. Cosmos' throat swelled. No one ever honestly wanted to keep him. At some point, he had begun pushing people away before they could push him away first. He always headed off rejection. For once, he saw a genuine connection unfolding in front of him. Becoming a vampire gave him an avenue to see what was real. Vega was real.

Cosmos took the bottle of cleaning solution that Vega held and set it aside. Next, he took Vega's hand towel and tossed it over his shoulder. His gaze never wavered from holding Vega's stare. He snagged Vega's hips and hauled him closer. Their lower bodies met. Vega gasped. Cosmos slid his hands down Vega's back until he cupped Vega's ass. He felt everything Vega felt. Cosmos heard his every thought. Their connection grew by the second. Vega's blood pumped through Cosmos' veins, sustaining him. Cosmos' fangs grew at the memory of Vega's flavor on his tongue.

"You came earlier when I bit you."

Vega's lips parted on a pant.

Cosmos moved against Vega, letting the friction between their bodies drive the heat between them. "Do you think it was because of where I bit you? I'm sure you didn't come when Aaron bit your wrist."

Vega scowled. "Of course not."

He was adorable when he got irritated. Cosmos smirked. "Well, then either it's bite placement, or it's me."

Vega's gaze dropped to Cosmos' mouth. He licked his lips. "Maybe we should try again... like an experiment."

"Hmmm. Where should I bite you next?" Cosmos asked, trying not to sound too excited. He wanted to bite until he drained Vega. Then he wanted to give Vega his blood so they could have eternity. The realization scared Cosmos a little. That didn't stop him from lowering his nose to Vega's shoulder. He inhaled. His lips moved upward, skimming Vegas's skin until he reached Vega's throat. The sound of Vega's pulse filled his ears. It sped with anticipation as Cosmos kissed Vega's pulse point. He licked. Vega panted. Cosmos' fangs scraped Vega's skin. Vega whimpered. Cosmos bit. Blood filled his mouth. Vega cried out in pleasure. His hand dove inside Cosmos' shorts. He stroked and tugged, pleasuring Cosmos as Cosmos drank. Cosmos sealed the wound but kept suckling Vega's skin as he rode Vega's palm. He lost himself in Vega's arms. He didn't know what would happen tomorrow. Cosmos had no clue if Vega's idea for his spin class would work. All he knew was all was right when Vega held him. For now, it was enough.

CHAPTER FOUR

FOR WEEKS, COSMOS SPENT each day sleeping in Vega's bed. He spent his nights swapping between following Aaron, working on Vega's idea for his spin class, and making love to Vega every chance he got. Cosmos felt strangely whole, despite his life being more unsettled than ever. He hadn't quite figured out how to launch a subscription service. His rent wasn't behind on the gym yet, but that was only because Cosmos had done a bit of shameless mind control on the bank manager over the phone. He was grateful to learn that was a skill he possessed. Cosmos didn't like how that made him feel, though. He wanted to succeed because he deserved it. It was a matter of pride.

The same delicious scent pulled him from a death sleep that did every night when the sun set. His stomach growled. Vega was his favorite meal. He had expected to miss food. Instead, the idea of putting actual food in his mouth made his stomach heave. But thinking of sucking down some Vega, that was another story. The guy was a delicacy.

Cosmos followed his nose and the steady sound of Vega's heartbeat. As always, he found a smiling Vega waiting. Vega came to his feet as Cosmos stepped inside the living room. Something swelled inside Cosmos' chest, the way it did every time he set eyes on Vega. Vega met him halfway with a kiss. Before they exchanged a word of greeting, Aaron's bedroom door opened.

His lip curled in disgust as he looked at them. "I'm going out."

"Okay. I love—" He was gone before Vega finished. Vega rubbed his forehead.

"I'll watch over him."

Vega nodded, but he looked defeated. For the first time, it truly hit Cosmos how much of a toll this life took on Vega. He was the one who kept watch all day while they slept. No one showed him an ounce of appreciation. Cosmos tried, but he doubted it made up for losing Vega's son. Vega kept a roof over the head of a grown man who gave zero fucks about anyone. It had to be exhausting. It had to be isolating as hell.

"I love you."

Cosmos didn't have a plan. The words just popped out. That didn't make them any less true. Vega was amazing. Cosmos didn't need months or even years of a growing connection. He just knew. Vega was the one. This was love.

Vega's lips parted. Then the sweetest smile Cosmos had ever seen exploded across his face. "I love you too."

Cosmos nodded. "When I get back, we should talk about that. But I have to keep your son safe first."

Vega visibly swallowed. "Okay. Please be careful."

"Of course. I'd never endanger my chances of coming home to you." He kissed Vega's forehead and zipped out behind Aaron before he lost him. It was odd for things to be so easy with Vega when everything had been so hard his entire life. But that was how Cosmos knew it was real. Vega brought him peace.

Normally, when Cosmos followed Aaron, Aaron found the closest human, grabbed a bite, and went back home. He never seemed to enjoy being out of his bedroom for long. Tonight, Aaron obviously had a destination in mind. The realization had the hair on the back of Cosmos' neck standing on end. Aaron headed for an apartment complex and directly to the second floor of the H building. Cosmos hid in the shadows and watched as Aaron nervously fidgeted with his clothes before knocking on door three. It was obvious he knew exactly who lived there.

A large dark-haired guy who blocked out the light of the room behind him opened the door. He didn't look happy to see Aaron. "What are you doing here, buddy?"

"I came to see my dad."

Cosmos had an immediate gut check reaction of dislike. He realized too late this was Aaron's other dad, Teddy. All Cosmos knew about the guy was his name and that he had left a twenty-year-long relationship with an amazing man for someone younger. That was it. He was bigger than Cosmos expected. Bear-like. Cosmos wanted to kick him in the balls.

Terry stepped outside and pulled the door closed behind him, obviously having no intention of inviting Aaron inside. He looked around. "Where's Vega? Shouldn't you be with him?"

A humorless laugh burst from Aaron. "I'm an adult, Dad. I don't need a leash."

Terry focused on Aaron. "It's pretty late, and you know Jarod doesn't like anything that reminds him of my age."

Cosmos winced.

"Namely your adult son." Aaron's voice sounded dead.

Terry nodded. "Mostly you."

Aaron didn't say a word. He turned and walked away.

"Aaron."

Aaron didn't look back when Terry called his name.

Cosmos waited until Terry went back inside before stepping from the shadows, catching up to Aaron and matching his stride. "So that's your other dad, huh?"

Aaron didn't look his way.

Cosmos felt the hurt and anger rolling off him in waves. He experienced something he didn't want to feel for Aaron: pity. Cosmos heard himself telling a story he never told. "My parents skipped out on my eighteenth birthday. They didn't even wait until the next day or until we had cake or anything. It was like they couldn't be done with parenting fast enough. They said they'd come back, but they never did."

"You could find them now. There's nothing stopping you. You're powerful. You can do anything you want now. Go anywhere. Hunt them down." There wasn't an ounce of emotion in Aaron's voice, but he was talking. Cosmos took it as a win.

"Nah. I'm thirty-four. If they had ever wanted me, they've known where to find me. I never left the shitty apartment they abandoned me in, even when the rent increases got out of control. No matter what, I stayed just in case they wanted to come back. You never grow out of wanting your parents to love you. But the truth is, while every child deserves parents, not every parent deserves a child. I think you probably have to let this one go."

Aaron snorted. "Why? Because I have you now?"

"No. I mean, you do have me, but that's not why. For sanity's sake."

Aaron snorted again.

Cosmos held his silence. He didn't know what else to say. In truth, he didn't know why he bothered in the first place. Aaron had stolen his life. He shouldn't care. The kid was a complete shithead, but then again, Cosmos had been the same way for a while after his parents left. Obviously, he hadn't gone on a spree of vampire-turning, but Cosmos had done his fair share of self-destructive things that had also hurt other people. He remembered what it had been like to be Aaron. But Aaron wasn't alone the way Cosmos had been, and Cosmos wouldn't let him forget that.

"Jarod isn't even hot. He's just young. What's up with that? Why would Terry leave us for him? Dad gave that asshole everything just for him to leave us for some guy who looks like his parents are first cousins."

Cosmos pressed his lips together to keep from laughing. He didn't dare make a sound. Aaron was talking, and he didn't want to break this new olive branch.

"What did you do to get past your parents leaving?"

The question surprised Cosmos. He answered honestly. "At first, I did a lot of terrible things, hurting a lot of people who didn't deserve it, and then I went to therapy."

"Therapy? Men go to therapy?"

A smile snapped to Cosmos' lips. "Of course. I've been going for years. Maybe not now since I sleep all day. But when I went, there were always tons of men in the waiting room, waiting for their turn."

Aaron nodded, looking thoughtful. "Dad says you're wanting to start an online spin class. I could help with that. I have a pretty big online following and my video editing skills are nothing to sneeze at. That's what I planned to do before my life got thrown off track by the vampirism thing. I wanted to work in digital media."

For the first time, Cosmos saw Aaron as a whole person rather than just the guy who had stolen his dreams. It was obvious Aaron lashed out at the world for having his future stolen from him on top of the issues with his dad. Cosmos understood, and he cared. Aaron was young. Cosmos wanted to be the adult he never had. "I'd love to have your help. I have no idea how to launch this subscription service. Since I can't hold daytime classes any longer, I won't be able to keep the doors open much longer on just night classes. I need to get the online thing rolling."

Aaron glanced his way. "I'm sorry." He sounded sincere, taking Cosmos by surprise. "It's a little embarrassing to admit, but I didn't actually mean to turn you. I just didn't want you to die after I took too much blood." He winced. "In fact, I never meant to turn anyone. No one taught me how to feed. I've just been winging it and I don't really like it. A few times, I've waited until I'm too hungry to control it, and then I'm too far gone. I never set out to intentionally ruin anyone's life."

Cosmos' chest hurt. Aaron seemed very young at that moment. He recognized Aaron was legally an adult, but he was too damn young to be a fucking vampire. "How did you end up like this?"

A humorless laugh burst from Aaron. "Stupidity." He ran his hand through his hair. "I let my friend talk me into going to this sketchy party at some dude's house. This incredibly hot guy spoke to me while I was there. At least, I think he was hot. I'm not sure if he was or if he only made me see what he wanted. Anyhow, my mind went kind of fuzzy. The next thing I know, we were alone in the bedroom, making out. Then I woke up alone in an abandoned house in a completely different neighborhood. The guy was gone, and I was left with no real memory of what happened other than just this nonstop feeling of something horrible out there waiting to pop up around every corner. It was the next night, and I had missed over sixty calls from Dad. He didn't even flinch, really."

"You're his son. He loves you no matter what."

Aaron nodded. "I know."

"You're lucky. I've never had anyone who wouldn't leave me the way he'd never turn his back on you." It was the only way

Cosmos could think to say Aaron should stop being a dick to his dad without saying Aaron should stop being a dick to his dad.

Then Aaron ripped the rug out from beneath him. "That's not true. You have Dad too. He loves you. I see the way he looks at you. Dad is loyal. He won't ever leave you either."

A terrible thought hit. He would grow old, though. Vega would die and Cosmos wouldn't. So, really, he would leave Cosmos eventually. The way everyone did. He didn't know where to go with this new revelation. Nothing mattered to him anymore as much as Vega. He couldn't fathom losing him. Cosmos shook his head. He wouldn't borrow trouble. Vega would grow old, and Cosmos would be at his side—like any normal couple. He wouldn't overthink things. Cosmos was happy. That was all that mattered. Everything else would take care of itself. He had to believe that. Otherwise, he might lose his mind.

Life with Cosmos was everything Vega ever wanted. When Aaron and Cosmos came through the door together, talking and laughing, Vega did his best to hide his surprise. Having his son back and having Cosmos and Aaron bonding were two dreams that felt completely out of his reach. Tonight was the first time he saw a glimmer of hope. Too bad it came at the end of all things.

Vega watched the smiles bleed from Cosmos and Aaron. Cosmos' face hardened. Aaron looked ready to cry. That last part almost broke Vega. He hadn't seen Aaron cry through any of this. Aaron had turned defiant the day his dad left. Turning vampire had only made him dig his heels deeper into bitterness. Seeing his eyes well with tears now was too much for Vega.

"It'll be okay."

"Shut up." The beast who held his throat tightened his grip, cutting off Vega's oxygen. His mind went wild as he fought for air.

It's okay, baby. I won't let you die.

The grip loosened on his neck and air filled his lungs. Vega tried to see through his watery eyes, but he was too busy fighting to survive.

"Do you remember me, baby boy?"

Vega's skin crawled at the perversion that weaved through the question. No one answered.

The stranger took his fury out on Vega's throat again. "Answer me before I kill the daddy who gave you life."

"Yes," Aaron rushed to answer, sounding shaky. "I remember you."

Vega wanted to cry. There had always been a small part of him that feared this day. He had always wondered about the monster who turned his son and if not knowing would come back to haunt them. Now he knew and it was so much worse than anything his baby had confessed. His heart ached at the idea of what his son had endured in silence.

"Then why haven't you come to me? It's been forever. I've been patient. I tried to let you grow up and have a little fun with the gift I gave you, but you never came looking. Why didn't you come for me?" His voice became more desperate and pleading by the second. Vega lost hope with each word. There was a sickness inside this one. He wouldn't let anyone here live.

Stop, baby. No matter what, you won't die tonight. I have you.

Vega focused on Cosmos as the promise brushed his mind, and Vega knew what he had to do. For a while now, Vega had known he would have to become a vampire too. He couldn't stay human and stay with Cosmos and Aaron. Vega couldn't force them to watch him grow old and die, leaving them forever young. Aaron was one thing. It was natural to outlive his child, but eventually, the age difference between Cosmos and him would become an issue. His ex-husband had already given him a complex on the topic. He had already watched one man leave him for someone younger. Vega had been a bit scared to broach the topic, though. He honestly liked his humanity. Plus, he adored the biting aspect of his relationship with Cosmos. He didn't know if that would end when he turned. Vega would miss feeding Cosmos. But he would be damned if this perverted psycho hurt his child again. He couldn't let anything else happen to his baby.

"Answer me!" The roar at Vega's back made him jump. His heart tried climbing into his throat.

Vega met Cosmos' stare.

Cosmos gave him a subtle nod and Vega knew Cosmos had been listening to his every thought. It was time. He punched behind him as hard as possible, aiming for the vampire's balls. Pain was all he knew as his throat collapsed beneath the vampire's hold. He dropped, gasping with no hope. A spray of blood arched through the air as Cosmos moved too fast for the human eye and tore the throat from their intruder.

Aaron's face appeared over him. Tears streamed down his face. "It's okay, Dad. I've got you. I won't let anything happen to you." Aaron bit his wrist and then tried smearing blood on Vega's lips. Everything had a desperate and surreal hue. Life got darker around the edges by the second.

Cosmos appeared on his other side. His face was covered in so much blood, he was unrecognizable. Vega might have heaved if his throat wasn't crushed.

"This isn't working." Aaron's cry sounded far away.

Cosmos responded, but Vega could no longer hear. "I love you," he mouthed, hoping the pair understood he meant it for them both. They were the best part of him. He was glad they had each other. Cosmos would make sure his son wasn't alone. That was all Vega could ask. That was all he needed to know to let go, and he knew with all his heart Cosmos would never let him down. He was free to move on.

CHAPTER FIVE

SOMETHING SMELLED AMAZING. VEGA moved closer to it. He hunted the scent in the dark. Exhaustion kept his eyes shut, but his body gravitated toward the delicious aroma. Vega licked his lips. He was so parched. The inside of his mouth felt the Sahara. Warm lips touched his. A happy hum rose in his throat. He should have known only Cosmos would smell like hot chocolate with marshmallows and some kind of spice that Vega wanted filling his mouth. His body kept moving until he straddled Cosmos.

A sexy chuckle rumbled against his lips. Cosmos squeezed his ass, drawing him closer. Vega didn't recall going to bed, but he loved waking up like this. He bit Cosmos' bottom lip. Cosmos gasped. Blood filled Vega's mouth. Vega swallowed and froze. Everything came flashing back at the speed of absolute terror. The shaking set in and Cosmos' hold tightened on him.

"Shhh. It's okay, gorgeous. I have you."

With his face buried in the crook of Cosmos' neck, Vega listened to the blood rushing through Cosmos' veins. He forcibly drew his mind back until he only heard Cosmos' heartbeat, and then again until only Cosmos' breathing filled his ears. The more control he took of his senses, the calmer he became.

"You saved me."

"It was a team effort, really. Aaron drained your blood, and I gave you mine."

Vega smiled. "It was good to see you laughing with my son before everything went to shit." Vega had to talk about that, because he couldn't talk about dying. Not yet.

Cosmos stroked his back. Vega felt him shrug. "He's a good kid."

A wave of emotion washed over Vega that had him fighting back tears. No one had called his son good in a long time, even though Vega had never stopped believing it. Terry had left them, and Aaron had lost his way, but Aaron had been a damn good kid. Vega had known that person was still inside Aaron. It meant everything that Cosmos saw that too.

"What will my life be like now?"

Cosmos shifted beneath him. He touched Vega's chin, forcing Vega to meet his stare. "You'll spend it with me. You'll spend it with your son. Everything else, we'll figure out together."

Vega took a breath. He forced himself to stay focused on Cosmos. If he looked too much at the big picture, he wanted to hyperventilate. Instead, he chose to stay in the moment. "Will I spend it with you?"

A line appeared between Cosmos' eyebrows. "Of course. I told you I was marrying you. I told you I love you."

Vega didn't know why, but he adored the cranky side of Cosmos. That side got shit done. That side took care of everything. "Now, come on. You're hungry and you need to learn how to feed. Pick where you want to bite me."

Confusion had Vega forgetting his worries. "Wait. I can feed from you? I don't need to bite humans?"

Cosmos shrugged. "Well, one of us will have to, but not this second. You can learn from me. I have enough blood to share right now."

Vega bit his bottom lip, feeling shy. He didn't want to hurt Cosmos, and he felt awkward trying new things.

Cosmos' fangs peeked out. "You won't hurt me. Don't you like it when I bite you?"

Vega nodded.

Cosmos' erection grew between them. "I want that too."

Damn. Vega needed to make Cosmos feel the way Cosmos made him feel when Cosmos fed from him. He sat back on his heels and eyed Cosmos' nude body. There were so many yummy options. That delicious smell overcame him again. Vega slithered lower. He leaned in and kissed Cosmos' stomach. Cosmos' heartbeat quickened. Vega relished the sound as he kissed a path down Cosmos' torso. He stopped to lick Cosmos' cock for a moment before moving on and sinking his fangs into Cosmos' thigh.

COSMIC CARDIO

A cry ripped through the air. Cosmos grabbed his hair and held on. Blood filled Vega's mouth. He drank. Vega had never been thirstier in his life. The smell of cum mixed with the sexy scent of Cosmos' blood. Vega sucked, wanting more.

"I don't want you to stop, but you have to, baby. If you take too much, I'll be too weak to hunt for myself."

Vega withdrew his fangs and licked the wound; the way Cosmos always did for him. The holes sealed and disappeared. Cosmos panted beneath him, covered in cum. Vega wanted more. In a flash, he had lube covering his fingers. He didn't know how it happened. Vega thought about what he wanted, and it appeared. He shoved Cosmos' thighs apart and fingered his asshole.

"I need to know if you'll feel different on my dick."

An evil-sounding chuckle rumbled from Cosmos. "You don't need an excuse to fuck me. I want it."

"Good." Vega impaled him with his cock.

Cosmos grabbed the headboard to keep from hitting his head from the force of the thrust. Everything felt realer. Rawer. It was like Vega had never seen, heard, or smelled the world before that moment. He had never fucked before that moment. There was one more thing he realized above all others.

"I've never had a love like yours." Cosmos loved him selflessly. Purely. Without an agenda or strings. Vega had never experienced that.

"Ours. It's our love. Not just mine." Cosmos snagged the back of Vega's neck and pulled him down for a kiss. As a blinding orgasm exploded through him, Vega realized eternity didn't sound so bad. He had the perfect family now. Together, the three of them could do anything. He hoped Cosmos felt the same.

I do, which is what you'll be saying as soon as we get moving for the night.

"We're getting married tonight?"

Cosmos kissed the tip of Vega's nose. "You're damn right we are. This family is mine."

Vega couldn't stop smiling. They were proof life didn't always turn out as planned, but life still had a plan, nonetheless. He absolutely believed they had

been written in the stars. They were cosmic.

CHAPTER SIX

"BREATHE IN AND RELEASE. Let's glide to a stop with a renewed spirit. And, until next time, please remember all of us at the Cosmic Cardio family believe in you." Cosmos had been delivering the same line for over a year, and it never got old. He loved this place.

Cosmos climbed from his bike and said his goodbyes to his usual members before making his way toward the back of the room. Before he could cut the camera, recording tonight's class, a new face stepped into his path. "Hi. I'm Jarod."

Despite being taken aback by Jarod's over-the-top enthusiasm, Cosmos pasted on a smile. He was always happy to greet a new client. "Hi, Jarod. It's nice to meet you." They shook hands.

Jarod didn't let go. "You may not know this, but I'm Aaron's stepdad. Well, sort of. His dad and I aren't officially married, but we've lived together for a few years now, so..."

Cosmos fought to keep his smile in place. He could easily snatch his hand away, but he didn't always know his own strength with humans. Cosmos didn't want to rip off the guy's arm. Well, he did, but he shouldn't. That would be frowned upon. "It seems I've heard the name."

Jarod's smile grew. "Oh, good. It might've been awkward, otherwise."

Yes, because this wasn't awkward at all. Cosmos tried to gently pry his hand away. "I'm thrilled you sought out my class." This wasn't creepy at all.

Jarod moved closer, still clinging to Cosmos' hand. "Actually, this is my third time here. I just usually zip out before I'm spotted. Would you like to get a drink?"

"Why?" Even Cosmos heard how repulsed he sounded by the idea.

Jarod shrugged. His gaze dropped to their joined hands. Cosmos got the impression the move was meant to be coy. It made Cosmos' stomach churn. One of Jarod's shoulders lifted in a half shrug. "I don't know. When Terry was married to Vega, he was bored as hell. I had a lot of fun making him not bored... if you know what I mean. I could do the same for you."

Cosmos snatched his hand away so fast, Jarod nearly fell on his face. "Ewww." Cosmos cleared his throat. "No seriously, ewwww. I mean this with all the disrespect I can muster, Vega is way, and I do mean *way* hotter than you. You should be thanking any goddess listening to you that Terry wanted you and run back home to him. Holy shit. The audacity."

The door opened and Terry strolled in, looking thunderous. "I thought I told you to stop coming to this class."

"I can't help it if you're jealous of me being around anyone younger than you."

COSMIC CARDIO

Cosmos rolled his eyes and headed for the back of the studio and stopped the recording. As he did so, a warm breeze washed over him along with a familiar delicious scent. A smile automatically snapped to Cosmos' lips. He knew without looking, Vega was there.

"What are you doing here?"

Cosmos turned at the ugliness snapped in Vega's direction from Terry. Vega looked every bit as shocked to have Terry and Jarod standing there as Terry looked to see him coming through the door.

"This is my husband's studio. Why are you here?"

Terry looked Jarod's way.

Cosmos winked at Vega. "Jarod came to offer to save me from my boring marriage the same way he saved Terry."

Vega's eyebrows rose.

Terry looked thunderous.

"I did no such thing. I had no clue this class had any connection to your ex."

Cosmos motioned to the camera behind him. "Actually, this camera was rolling the whole time. You're free to see for yourself."

"How entertaining," Vega said, stepping around everyone and heading for the digital recorder Aaron had set up for him.

"You're wasting your time." Jarod tried, dragging Terry toward the door. "He's just trying to start trouble."

Terry shook off his hold and followed them as Vega grabbed the device from its tripod.

"You won't have to go back far. This literally just happened before you two walked through the door." Cosmos was enjoying himself a little too much.

"Let's go, Terry," Jarod said, sounding firm. "This is getting ridiculous. If you don't leave with me now, we're done."

Vega hit play. Jarod's voice filled the room. "When Terry was married to Vega, he was bored as hell. I had a lot of fun making him not bored... if you know what I mean. I could do the same for you."

"Ewww." Cosmos looked at Vega. He hid a smile but kept watching the footage. "No seriously, ewwww. I mean this with all the disrespect I can muster, Vega is way, and I do mean *way* hotter than you. You should be thanking any goddess listening to you that Terry wanted you and run back home to him. Holy shit. The audacity."

"Go get in the truck."

"Terry."

"Go get in the truck!" At Terry's roar, Cosmos and Vega exchanged a glance.

Jarod scrambled for the door. Terry's gaze moved between them, as if searching for any hint of satisfaction, before landing on Vega. "How's Aaron?"

Vega moved closer to Cosmos. Cosmos took the hint and wrapped his arm around his waist. "He's good."

Terry's dark gaze moved between them again before meeting Vega's stare. "So, you're remarried."

It wasn't a question, but Vega still nodded. He motioned Cosmos' way. "This is Cosmos."

Terry didn't acknowledge the introduction. "You look great. I'd swear you're twenty years younger."

A tight smile touched Vega's lips. "It's just been that long since you've seen me happy."

Cosmos wondered for a moment if he would have to fight Terry. The man's rage was visibly real. After a moment, he gave Vega a sharp nod. "I suppose that's fair." Without another word, he walked away, leaving a silent Vega behind. Cosmos didn't know how to feel. In the year since Cosmos showed up on Vega's doorstep, Vega had never once closed his mind to Cosmos. The absolute lack of sound now made him wonder if he had gone deaf.

"Are you okay?"

Vega's gaze moved Cosmos' way and sound rushed back as Vega's suddenly reopened his mind to him. "Yeah, I'm good. Sorry. I just had an ugly moment."

"You can share those with me too. You don't have to keep those to yourself."

Vega shook his head and then nodded, as if still shaken by the encounter. "I know. I just... it's odd."

"What is?"

"I don't remember loving him."

Vega's confession was the last thing Cosmos expected, but Vega kept going.

"We have a son. He absolutely broke me when he left me and I don't remember feeling anything for him. When he was standing here, it was so fucking strange to think of him as even Aaron's dad. That's you. That's us. He asked about Aaron, and it was like a stranger asking. I think I either didn't love him or I didn't know love before you because he's no one."

Since Cosmos had a front-row seat to all of Vega's thoughts and emotions, he knew every word Vega said was true. He felt nothing for Terry. Their bond eclipsed anything humans experienced. It was eternal. Terry and Jarod seemed so insignificant and petty. Fleeting. Their lives would end one day, and their family would still stand strong millennia after every human currently living had turned to dust.

"He's nothing. He was just a bookmark while you waited for me."

Vega set the camera back on the tripod and crowded Cosmos' space. "What can I do to keep you from getting bored as hell with me?"

Irritation ran through Cosmos. "Don't you dare let that child of two first cousins get under your skin. There's nothing boring about you."

Vega snorted. "You're not the only one with a front-row seat to my thoughts and emotions. I have one to yours, remember? You might be a lot of things, but bored isn't one of them."

"Right? I can't keep up. People think these thick thighs are from all these spin classes, but really, it's from riding that dick."

Vega laughed just like Cosmos hoped he would. Now all Cosmos needed to do was make Vega moan, just like he planned for him to. Then Cosmos would keep Vega smiling for the rest of eternity, just like he vowed to do. The perfect plan come to fruition.

Keep an eye out for the next Once Upon a Bite, *Must be Clowning Me.*

Please consider leaving a review at the retailer where you purchased this book. Reviews really help with a book's visibility, which allows me to continue writing more stories. Thank you, Charity.

ABOUT THE AUTHOR

CHARITY PARKERSON IS AN award-winning and multi-published author with several companies. Born with no filter from her brain to her mouth, she decided to take this odd quirk and insert it in her characters. One of her greatest loves is writing morally gray characters. You'll find them scattered throughout her hundreds of titles.

*Eight-time Readers' Favorite Award Winner

COSMIC CARDIO

*2015 Passionate Plume Award Finalist

*2013 Reviewers' Choice Award Winner

*2012 ARRA Finalist for Favorite Paranormal Romance

*Five-time winner of The Mistress of the Darkpath

Connect with her online:

*Sign up for her newsletter: https://sendfox.com/charityparkerson

*Join her readers' group on Facebook: http://bit.ly/CharitysTribe

*Website: https://www.charityparkerson.com

*A list of her social media accounts and giveaways all in one place: http://hy.page/charityparkerson